MW01075325

CATHOLIC STORIES
FOR
BOYS AND GIRLS

Volume I

The stories herein are republished in the hope that in a small way the Faith, Culture and Tradition of the Holy Roman Catholic Church may be preserved for our most prized possession, our children.

May our Divine Lord bless each boy and girl who reads these stories, as well as every one who helps to place them in their hands.

MICHAEL J. CURLEY
Archbishop of Baltimore.

Catholic Stories for Boys and Girls Volume I

Published by Neumann Press, an imprint of TAN Books.
Books. Originally published as: "Catholic Stories for Boys
and Girls—Volume I," 1992." Revised edition with color
corrections, cover design copyright © Neumann Press.

ISBN: 978-0-911845-46-4

Printed and bound in the United States of America.

Neumann Press
Charlotte, North Carolina
www.NeumannPress.com

2014

CATHOLIC STORIES
for
BOYS and GIRLS

Stories written and compiled in days long past
by Catholic nuns in America and dedicated to
Mary the Mother of God
our dear Lady of the Miraculous Medal

NEUMANN PRESS
Charlotte, North Carolina

Come, Holy Spirit!

The Best Deed

I

Our Lady wears both blue and white,
Her hands hold rays of golden light.

The Confirmation Class was quite large. There were as many boys as girls in it. They were sitting in a big hall. Sister Rose was talking to them. On her desk there was something. It was covered with a white cloth. Sister said:

"Confirmation Day will be here soon. You are trying to get ready for this great day, I know. You come to every class. You know your Catechism.

"Today we will talk about another way

of getting ready. But first, I have something nice to show you."

Sister pulled the white cover away. The
children's eyes got very big. They smiled.
On Sister's desk was a beautiful statue of
our Lady. She wore a white robe and a
blue veil. She was holding out her hands.
Golden rays were falling from her hands.
Sister Rose said:

"This beautiful statue was sent to me
from France. It came across the sea in a
big ship. Can you guess what I am going
to do with it? Well, I am going to tell you.
On Confirmation Day, I am going to give
this beautiful statue away. I am going to
give it to one of you boys or girls."

All the boys and girls said, "Oh!"

8

Sister went on:

"You are all getting ready to be confirmed. You are getting your souls ready for God the Holy Ghost! You are getting ready to be soldiers of Christ. You must try to love our Lord very much. You must do things to please Him. The boy or girl who does the best deed before Confirmation Day will have this beautiful statue.

"The day before Confirmation each one of you must bring me a little letter. In the letter you must tell me your good deed. You must not tell any one else what it is. Only God must know. That is all.

"Now you may go."

O Holy Spirit, come I pray,
And help me to do good each day.

II

In the Confirmation Class there was a little girl named Catherine Duffy. She had blue eyes and golden curls. Her father was a doctor. He was very wise and kind. Catherine had three little brothers.

She thought very hard on her way home today. She wanted to win the beautiful statue of our Lady. She was thinking:

"What shall I do for a good deed?"

She thought and thought and thought. At the dinner table Catherine told about the statue of our Lady.

"What do you think would be the best deed to do?" she asked.

"Give up candy," said her little brother David. He liked candy very much.

"Make a visit to our Lord every day in the Church," said Benedict. He was an altar boy.

"Eat fish on Fridays," said Paul. Everybody laughed. They knew Catherine did

not like fish. Paul did not, either.

"Why not save your pennies for the little Chinese?" said Mother.

"Help me at St. Mary's Hospital," said Daddy. And everybody laughed again.

Catherine thought and thought. At last she made up her mind. She would give up candy. She liked candy better than even David did. To give up candy would be hard.

What is the best deed I can do,
To show, O God, my love for you?

11

III

Doctor Duffy was just getting in his car. Catherine was playing in front of the house. He called to her:

"I am going down to the hospital." Catherine ran over and jumped into the car with her Daddy. She knew the Sisters of Charity at St. Mary's Hospital. They were dressed in blue and white. They wore white cornettes on their heads. The white cornettes made Catherine think of white birds flying. She liked the Sisters. She used to watch them going to see the poor people in their own homes. Many poor people used to go to the Hospital, and the Sisters took care of them. Catherine had been to the Hospital many times.

Today Daddy had to see many sick people. So Catherine went to talk to Sister Gertrude. She was the Head Sister. Sister Gertrude was just going upstairs. So Catherine went with her. They walked down the halls and went through several

big rooms. Sister Gertrude was very kind
to the sick people. She made them feel
better.

They came to a big room where there
were some sick men. Catherine saw a
man with black hair and big black eyes.
He did not seem to be a very nice man.
He was talking to the nurse. Catherine
heard him say some curse words. Her
eyes got very big. She knew it was a bad
thing to say curse words. She walked over
to the foot of the bed. She stood looking
at him. The man saw her standing at the
foot of the bed. She said:

"You said some curse words. That is
not right."

The man did not say anything. He only

looked at her and smiled a little. Catherine went over a little closer. She said:

"Tell God that you are sorry and He will forgive you."

The man said:

"God hasn't much use for me. I often talk that way."

Catherine said:

"You won't go to Heaven if you talk like that. I wish you wouldn't."

She wanted to say:

"If you don't get sorry you will go to Hell," but she thought that maybe this would not be polite. The man guessed what she was thinking about. He said:

"It is no use, little girl. Maybe I could stop cursing, if you stayed around here."

Catherine looked at him very hard, then she said:

"I'll tell you what I am going to do. I am going to bring you my little statue of the Sacred Heart. I am going to put it by your bed. Every time you feel like cursing, just look at our Lord and say, 'My Jesus, mercy'."

Just then Daddy came into the room. He said:

"It is late. We must go right away."

And so they went home.

The next day Catherine took her statue of the Sacred Heart to the poor sick man. He smiled when she came to his bedside. She wanted to ask him if he had said any more curse words since yesterday. But she did not. She asked him how he was feeling. Then she said:

"Did you go to confession?" The man shook his head.

"I have not been to confession since I made my first Holy Communion," he said.

"Oh!" said Catherine. The tears came to her eyes. "My poor bad man! How black your soul must be! Why don't you get it all washed white again? Tell God you are sorry and tell your sins to the priest. God will forgive you."

The man shook his head again.

"I have been too bad," he said. "God does not love me any more."

"Yes, He does," said Catherine. "He died on the cross to save poor bad people like you."

Then she said:

"Maybe you don't remember. The next time I come, I am going to bring my station pictures."

The next day, when Daddy went to take her home, he found her sitting by the poor man's bed. She was showing him the

station pictures. She was holding one end of the long paper and he had the other end. She said to Daddy:

"We are just through. I was showing him how our Lord loves him."

She said to the man:

"Keep the pictures. I have to go home now."

The Sister said to Daddy:

"I am so glad that Catherine is coming every day to see this poor man. She seems to make him feel so much better. He hasn't any friends and he is not going to live very long. He will not be nice to any-one but Catherine."

Daddy told Mother all about it.

You should be kind to everyone, Our Lord has
   said, you see,
That "What you do to others, you do it unto
   Me."

IV

Every day Catherine went to see the poor sick man. Her mother would give her something to take to him. One day she would take him something good to eat. Another day she would take him some pretty flowers. Every day she would say to Sister Alice:

"Did he go to Confession?"

And Sister Alice would say:

"Not yet."

Then Catherine would say:

"How is he?"

And Sister would answer:

"Not very well."

Sister Alice used to take soup and other nice things to the poor.

One day Sister Alice gave Catherine a Miraculous Medal. She said:

"Maybe he will wear it for you. You know our Blessed Lady said that she would give great graces to those who wore this Medal."

That day the poor man seemed very

sick and very sad. Catherine said to him:

"Don't you want me to send for Father?"

And he said:

"I am too bad; God will not forgive me."

She said:

"Once there was a woman. She had done lots of bad things. She took some nice perfume and poured it on our Lord's feet. She dried them with her lovely golden hair. She cried for her sins. Our Lord forgave her."

Then she pinned the Medal on him. But he would not say anything more, so Catherine went home. She felt sad. She knew the poor man would die very soon.

In her room there was a pretty little altar. Over the altar hung a beautiful picture. It was a picture of our Lord when He was a little Boy. He was standing on a hillside. He was holding his Arms out very wide. Under the picture it said:

"This is how much I love you."

Catherine loved this picture very much. She said her morning and night prayers before it. Today she knelt down before it. She said:

"Dear Lord, I know You love this poor bad man, but I can't make him know You

as You really are. Please help me to make him know You. You are so kind. You are so good. He thinks You won't forgive him. But that is because he doesn't know any better."

She said to our Blessed Lady:

"I put your Miraculous Medal on him, so I am sure that you will help him."

Then she said the Rosary.

On a table was a lovely little bottle of perfume. Her Daddy had brought it to her from France, for he had been across the big sea. Catherine liked it very much. She did not like to give it away. But today, when she looked at it, she knew just what she was going to do with it.

When she went to the hospital in the

morning, she took the little bottle with her. She took it to the poor sick man and said:

"I have brought you this nice perfume. It came from France. Now you can pour it on our Lord's feet and tell Him you are sorry."

She pulled out the cork and gave him the bottle. He smelled it.

"Yes, it is nice," he said.

Catherine put the little statue of the Sacred Heart close to him.

"Now pour it on our Lord's feet. Tell Him you are sorry for your sins. He will forgive you."

The poor man thought a little. Then he leaned over and poured the perfume on our Lord's feet. He smiled at Catherine.

"You win," he said. "Go and get the priest."

Catherine was so glad! She ran to find the nurse.

"Nurse, nurse," she said, "the poor sick man wants the priest. He wants to go to Confession!"

The nurse sent for Father right away. She fixed the little table by the sick man's bed. She made it look like a little altar. She put on it two lighted candles and a crucifix.

Then Father came. Everybody went away and left Father with the poor sick man. He heard the confession of the poor sick man. Father gave him absolution. His soul was not black any more. It had been made white again. All his sins had been washed away by the Blood of our Lord.

Then Catherine came back into the room. She knelt at the foot of the bed.

She saw Father give the poor sick man Holy Communion. Our Lord came into his heart.

Then Father took the Holy Oil. He made the Sign of the Cross with it on the poor man many times, on his closed eyes; on his ears; his nose; his mouth; his hands; and his feet. Each time Father said, "Through this holy unction and His tender mercy may our Lord forgive you." Catherine knew that Father was giving him the beautiful Sacrament of the dying.

When she went home she was not sad any more about the poor sick man. She told her mother all that had happened. Her mother was glad, too. Her mother said:

"Did you write your letter to Sister Rose? In three days you will be Confirmed."

Catherine was surprised. She had forgotten about the letter. She went up to
her room. She sat down at her little desk.
This is what she wrote:

Dear Sister Rose:

I am sorry I did not do very much. Some
other boy or girl will get the statue of our
Lady. I did not do very much. I only gave
away a little statue of our Lord and a
bottle of perfume that Daddy brought
from France.

I was not going to eat candy, but I for-
got. I ate some. You see, I was thinking
about a poor, bad, sick man. I was very
busy helping him to get to Heaven.

With love,

Catherine Duffy.

Just then Catherine heard the phone
ring. Catherine was folding her letter,

when her mother came into the room. She came over and kissed Catherine. She said:

"Your poor sick man just died. Just before he died he told the nurse to thank you for being so kind to him. She said he kissed the Medal you put on him. She just called up."

Catherine thought a little. Then she picked up her pen. She unfolded the letter; she wrote:

"P. S. The poor sick man just went to Heaven. Nurse just told us."

V

Catherine went to Church on Confirmation Day with Mother and Daddy. She had on a white dress, white shoes and stockings. Over her head was a beautiful white veil. She had on a pretty wreath of white flowers. All the little girls wore white, and all the little boys wore dark blue. There were many people in the Church.

Mother and Daddy saw Catherine kneel at the feet of the Bishop. They knew that the Holy Spirit was coming into her soul to make her a soldier of Christ.

Her Mother said: "Dear Holy Spirit, please make Catherine good always."

Her Daddy said: "Dear Holy Spirit, keep my little girl as she is today."

Her little brothers were saying the "Hail Mary."

Catherine was very happy. She said: "Now I am a real soldier of Christ." Then she said: "O God, You know I wanted that statue of our Blessed Mother, but I am glad that poor man went to Heaven."

When Confirmation was over, they went to the class room. They were going to hear who won the statue. Sister Rose said:

"I have read all your letters. I am very pleased with them all. I am so pleased with all of you, that I am going to take every one on a big picnic next week."

All the boys and girls clapped their hands. Then Sister Rose said:

"God is very happy when we do little things to please Him. It is good to give up candy, and it is good to make visits to our Lord in Church. It is good, too, to save up pennies for the little pagan children. But the very best deed that I read

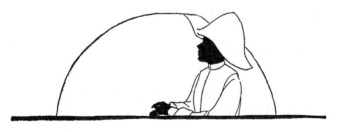

of, was about a little girl who helped a poor sick man to save his soul and get to Heaven.

"Catherine Duffy, come and get your statue."

Sister Rose was smiling.

Catherine's eyes got bigger and bigger. All the children clapped again. She walked up to the desk. Sister Rose put her arms around her and kissed her. Then she put the beautiful statue of our Lady in Catherine's arms.

What is the best thing we can do
To help save souls for love of You?

The Wreath of Flowers

I

The sun is shining, the day is bright;
And flowers nod in the morning light.

Once there was a little boy named Angelo. He lived in a country where it was summer all the year 'round. There were always many flowers. And if the sun didn't shine every day, it tried its best just the same. Angelo did not know what winter was like. He never saw snow or ice. He never felt a cold wind. Jack Frost never bit his nose. He never had to stay in the house to keep warm. But once he stayed in the house for three long weeks. And this is why.

Angelo was very ill. Every day he seemed worse. His mother took good care of him. She stayed with him night and day. But he did not get better. His poor mother cried. At last she said to herself:

"The Mother of God will make my child well if I pray to her."

She picked Angelo up and carried him out into the garden. She walked down the path. She came to a beautiful statue of our Lady.

Angelo's mother knelt down in front of the statue of our Lady. She laid Angelo on the ground at our Lady's feet. She said:

"Holy Mary, Mother of God, my little child is very sick. Please make him well again. You loved your little Baby Jesus. You know how bad I feel because Angelo is so ill. If you make him well again I will tell him that he must always love you very much. I will teach him to show his love for you every day."

Just as she said the last words to our Lady, Angelo opened his eyes and smiled

at her. He was well again. Our Lady had made him well. His mother was so happy. She picked him up and kissed him. She told him:

"The Mother of God has made you well again. You must love her very much."

Angelo was very happy, too.

Oh, you must love our Lady fair.
She keeps you in her loving care.

II

Every evening after that, Angelo used to go out into the garden and pick many beautiful flowers. He would make them into a wreath of flowers. He would take them to the beautiful statue of our Lady and put the wreath at her feet. Then he would kneel down and say:

"Holy Mother of Jesus, and my Mother, I give you this wreath of flowers to show you that I love you. I thank you for all you have done for me. Help me to keep my soul white. Bless my mother and my father."

Then he would say the "Hail Mary."

When he had said his prayers he would sit down near the beautiful statue of our Lady and look at her. He liked to sit and think about her. Then he would get up and throw her a kiss and run away.

Oh, let us gather flowers sweet,
And lay them at our Lady's feet.

III

The years came and went, and Angelo grew up. He loved our Lady very much — more now than he did when he was a little boy. He had never forgotten to make a wreath of flowers for our Lady every day.

One evening he came into the house and went to his mother.

"Dear Mother," he said, "I must go away."

"Angelo," said his mother, "what do you mean?"

"I must go away. Our Lady wishes me to be a Brother. High up among the great mountains there is a house where the Fathers and Brothers of St. Dominic live. They wear white all the time. Our Lady wishes me to go and live there. She wishes me to pray and do good deeds all my life."

Angelo's mother was both glad and sorry. She did not like to have him go away. She loved him very dearly, but she was glad that our Lady wished him to be a holy Brother. The big tears came into her eyes, but she smiled and said:

"Blessed be God and our dear Lady! I am so glad, Angelo." Then she kissed him.

Oh, go my son; our Lady calls.
Go serve her in the Brother's halls.

IV

And so Angelo went up, up, up among the mountains. He became a Brother. He was very happy. But one day Father James saw that Brother Angelo was not so happy. He saw as the days went by that Brother Angelo seemed very sad. And so Father James said to him one day:

"Brother Angelo, why are you so sad? You were so happy when you first came

to us. You are not happy now. Tell me
what I can do to make you happy again."

Brother Angelo was standing by the
window. He said:

"Father James, look out the window
and tell me what you see."

Father James was surprised when
Brother Angelo said this. But he looked
out the window and said:

"I see only the snow falling. The wind
is blowing it all about. I see snow and ice
everywhere I look. It is in the valleys and
on the mountain tops. But that is not
strange. It is always cold up here. We
have snow and ice all the year 'round."

"Yes," said Brother Angelo, "that is
just what I mean. That is why I am sad.

"In the country where I lived until I
came here, I saw only summer. Every
evening since I was just a little child, I
gathered flowers and made a wreath for
our Lady. I used to put it at the foot of
her beautiful statue in the garden. But
since I have been here I have not given
her even one wreath of flowers. Every

evening I feel sad because I think I cannot show my love for her as I used to."

Father James put his hand inside his white robe. He took out a Rosary. He held it out to Brother Angelo.

"Take this Rosary, my dear Brother," he said, "and do not be sad any more. This is a wreath of flowers that our dear Lady loves much more than those you used to give her. When you say the prayers of our Lady's Rosary, every 'Our Father' and every 'Hail Mary' changes into a beautiful rose in Heaven. The Angels take them and make them into a crown. They give it to our Lady. She is more pleased because these heavenly flowers are much more beautiful than those you used to give her. And then, too, these flowers do not fade, but bloom forever."

Brother Angelo took the Rosary and kissed it. He was happy again, because every day he could make a beautiful heavenly wreath of flowers for our Lady.

Rosary flowers more beautiful are
Than even sun, or moon, or star.

V

One day Father James had a letter to send to another House of St. Dominic, far, far away. He did not know how to send the letter. At last he said to himself:

"I shall send Brother Angelo and another Brother with this letter."

And so Brother Angelo and Brother Joseph left the mountains. They walked for many days. They came to a big woods. They walked on through it. They had nearly reached the other side when Brother Angelo said:

"Brother Joseph, it is nearly evening. Let us sit on this log and rest a little."

So they sat on the log to rest. Then Brother Angelo said:

"Brother Joseph, the sun is setting. Let us say our Rosary. This is the hour that I always make a wreath of heaven flowers for our Lady."

They did not see two men all in black coming softly behind them. These men were very bad. They were robbers. They would kill people going through the woods, and then take anything they had. Each man had a great big sharp knife. They came closer and closer very softly. They lifted their knives to strike. But just then everything became black. They could not see anything. They stopped still. Then a bright, bright light appeared. The robbers saw not only the two Brothers, but also many beautiful Angels. These were making a wreath of lovely white roses. Right in the middle of the Angels, was a Beautiful Lady. The Angels gave her the lovely wreath of white roses. Then the robbers heard Brother Angelo say:

"Brother Joseph, let us say another Rosary for men who do not love our Lady. We will ask her to make some bad men good again. We will ask her to make them sorry for their sins."

The Brothers began to pray again. And again the Angels began to make a wreath of roses. This time the roses were red. The two robbers looked and looked. They thought of all the sins they had done. They thought how black their souls were. They thought how good God and our Lady had been to them, and how bad they had been. They dropped their knives and hung their heads. They said:

"O God have mercy on us! Holy Mary, pray for us."

When they looked up they did not see our Lady or the Angels any more. They only saw the two Brothers praying. The

Brothers heard the robbers' prayer. They stood up and turned around to see where the words came from. The two robbers knelt at their feet. They told the Brothers how bad they had been, but that they wished to be good again.

Brother Angelo said:

"God will make your souls white again. Our dear Lady will pray for you."

He showed them the Crucifix.

"God died on the cross to save your souls. You must love Him very much and never be bad any more."

And so the robbers left the woods. They went with the Brothers. They went to Confession. Their sins were all washed by our dear Lord's Blood.

Brother Angelo knew that the prayers of the Rosary had saved their souls. He gave each of them a Rosary, and showed them how to say it. They loved it very much, and said it every day. They lived good lives after that. They never went back to the woods again.

Brother Angelo saved their souls when he said the Rosary.

Souls that are black, make white again,
O Queen of the Rosary. Amen.

Pedro of the Water Jars

I

I saw three ships a-sailing, a-sailing on the sea,
And, oh, how much I wished that one of them
were taking me!

I was very tired. I was hot and sleepy.
All day I had walked through the streets.
I had cried:

"Cold water! Nice cold water from the
deep well. Only a penny a cup. Nice water,
cold as ice."

Sometimes people listened to me and
took a cup. But there were not so many
today. All the people seemed very busy.
And I knew why. Tomorrow the three
ships would sail from Palos. Over a

May God Keep You Safe!

hundred men were going with the great leader, Columbus. They were going to sail away, away, for many, many days. They were going to the other side of the world. They would sail until they came to land on the other side of the world.

The women and children were crying. Their brothers or fathers or husbands were going. Everybody but the great leader, Columbus, and a few of his friends were afraid. They thought that the ships would never come back. Nobody had ever been so far before. They were afraid of many things.

Many times I had gone down to the water and looked at the three ships — the Pinta, the Nina and the Santa Maria. This last means Holy Mary.

I was not afraid. I wanted to go. But when I asked:

"Will any boys go?" the sailors laughed at me.

They said:

"Only big men go in this trip."

Even many of the big men were afraid.

I did not want to go home this evening. I did not have many pennies. The man whom I called my father would beat me if I did not bring home many pennies at night. I did not like my home. It was not a nice place. It was a small, dirty room. The man did not give me nice things to eat. He made me wear old clothes that did not fit me.

Every morning he made me get up very early. I had to fix the two big brown jars on the side of the little mule. I had to walk very far outside of Palos to a big well. I had to fill the two big jars with the cold water. Then I had to come back to Palos and walk through the streets with the mule. I sold the cold water to the people.

I did not want to go home tonight. Many times I had said to myself:

"I do not think that man is my father. He is so mean." Once I asked him:

"Where is my mother?"

He laughed and said:

"You will never see her again."

He would not say any more.

Sometimes, before I went to sleep at night, I seemed to remember other places and other people. They were beautiful places, and kind people. I seemed to remember a lovely garden. There were paths where I ran and played. I seemed to remember a beautiful house and many servants. There was a lady with beautiful dark hair and eyes. She had a lovely smile. I tried hard to remember these things, but they seemed so far, far away, like a dream — a very beautiful dream.

Tonight I was very tired. I stopped at the big Church. I always went there every evening, before I went home. I would go up and kneel before the Altar. I talked to our Lord. I asked Him to help me to be good. It was very hard sometimes. Then I would kneel before the statue of our Lady. I would ask her to bless me.

The Fathers of St. Francis showed me how to be good. They wear brown with a piece of white cord for a belt. They live in a big house on the hill. Father Juan was always kind to me. He is the Head Father.

It was nice and cool in the big Church. It was very quiet. I looked up in our Lady's face. I told her I was tired, and hot, and hungry. I asked her to help me.

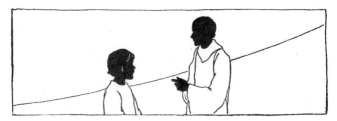

Just then a new thought came into my mind. If I could only get away from that bad man who said he was my father!

I could hear some of the sailors. They were talking outside the Church. I thought, "If I could only go away on a big ship." I knew they would not let boys go.

I think it was then that our Lady showed me what to do.

I went home. The man who said he was my father beat me; I did not care. I took a piece of bread and went to bed.

The next morning I left very, very early. I went to the well. I filled my water jars. I picked many beautiful, red flowers. I made a wreath for the big neck of each jar. Then I went to the Church. I took the two big jars to our Lady's altar.

I was nearly twelve years old. I was quite strong.

I said:

"O beautiful Mother of God, I give you these jars. I thank you for showing me what to do. Please take care of me."

I had left the little mule tied near the Church. Then I went out. I went down near the big ships.

The great leader, Columbus, and all his men went to Holy Mass that morning. They wanted to beg the blessing of God and our Lady. They went to Confession and received Holy Communion. I did not go. I waited until everybody had gone to Church. Then I went to one of the big ships. It was the Santa Maria. When nobody was looking I went on the ship. I had a very hard time doing this.

I went down inside the ship. It was dark. I hid behind a big box and a pile of rope. I was a little afraid. But I was not so hungry. I had a big piece of bread with me. I had some water, too.

I stayed there a long, long time. It was hot. I drank some water. I heard the men come. I heard them call to one another. Then the ship began to move. After a while I fell asleep.

God and our Lady keep you safe till you come home again,
From half the way around the world and golden lands. Amen.

II

I do not know how long I was hidden behind the box. I waked and slept and waked again. I ate some bread and drank a little water. I could hear the waves beat against the boat. I could hear the men talking and walking around. I wanted to get up and walk. But I did not dare to do so. One of the men came to get the rope on the box. He had a light. He saw me. He made me come out. The other sailors were there. I could look around and see water everywhere.

The men were angry with me. They said they were going to whip me. They were shouting.

Then I heard a kind voice say:

"Whom have you there?"

The men let me go and stood back. I saw a man with white hair, but he did not seem very old. He was richly dressed. He wore a gold chain. I knew it was the great leader, Don Columbus. I ran and knelt at his feet.

He said:

"Come with me."

He took me into a little room. He was very kind. I told him everything. He said:

"I am not angry with you. You may wait on me. You may be my cabin boy. I will take care of you."

This made me very glad.

After this the sailors were kind to me.

We sailed and sailed. Every evening we sang a hymn to our Lady. It was called "Star of the Sea." Nearly every day the sun shone. The sky was blue. I liked being on the ship very much. Soon we came to some land. On the land was a big hill. Fire came out of the top of it. The sailors were afraid, but Don Columbus was not.

Don Columbus was very nice to me. In the evening he let me stay on deck with him. I loved to sit with him and watch the bright stars come out. Don Columbus asked me many things. I think he felt sorry for me when I told him why I ran away. He would always say, "Trust in God and all will be well."

Sometimes I would ask him things, and he would tell me what I wanted to know. He told me he had tried for many years to get ships and money. He went to Kings and Princes of other countries. But they would not help him.

At last he came to Spain. He told me that he had stopped at the house of the Fathers of St. Francis in Palos. He was very tired. My Father Juan had been very kind to him.

Father Juan found out that Columbus wanted ships and money. He said:

"I know the good Queen Isabella. I will tell her all about you and what you want to do."

Good Father Juan got on his mule and rode off to see the Queen. He told her what Columbus wanted. Our good Queen Isabella said:

"I will help him."

Then she said that Columbus could be called "Don."

Only very great men in my country may be called "Don."

"But why do you want to go to the other side of the world?" I asked.

Don Columbus said:

"Pedro, there are very many people over there who do not know about God.

We want to take to them the light of our Holy Faith. The good Queen Isabella and Father Juan and I want to help them to save their souls.

"We want to find out about some other things, too."

Don Columbus said we were going to a beautiful country. We would find much gold there. We would see many rich people living in large cities.

I asked him about what I had heard the sailors say. They had told me that the earth was flat. And when our ship came to the end, it would fall off the world. I asked him if this were true.

Don Columbus laughed. He said:

"No, Pedro, the earth is not flat. The earth is round like a ball. We cannot fall off. We are sailing around it."

"But what about the big fishes that can

eat our ships and all the sailors?" I said.

Don Columbus laughed again.

"There are no such fishes. And there aren't any queer people in the water, either."

"But," I said, "the sailors say we shall come to a place where the sea is boiling hot. They say the ships will catch fire and burn up."

You see, I was a little afraid.

Don Columbus said:

"Do not listen to the things that the sailors tell you. They do not know what they are talking about."

Then I felt better. I always believed what Don Columbus said.

Another evening we were sitting on the deck. I was near Don Columbus. He was passing his hand over my head. I liked him to do that. He said:

"I know a lady who had a little boy. She loved him very much. They lived in a beautiful home. They had many servants. One of the servants was bad. He took the little boy one night. He ran away with him. His poor mother cried and cried. Everybody looked and looked for the little boy."

"Did they ever find him?" I asked.

"No," said Don Columbus, "not yet. But maybe some day they will."

"Was his mother beautiful?" I asked again. "Did she have big, dark eyes and a lovely smile?"

"Yes, she has big, dark eyes and a lovely smile."

"That is like the lady in my dreams," I said.

"Tell me about her," said Don Columbus.

And so I told him of how I seemed to remember a lady with the dark eyes and a beautiful smile. I told him about beautiful gardens and the big house, too. I felt very sorry for the little boy whom the bad

servant had taken away. He must have loved his beautiful home and his lovely mother. I said so.

"Well," said Don Columbus, "the little boy's mother prays a great deal. Every day she asks our dear Lady to help her find her little son. Our Lady loves boys very much. She loves mothers, too. She hears their prayers."

I liked Don Columbus very much.

We sailed on and on. We came to a place all covered with sea weed. Then the wind blew for days and days. We had been sailing nearly a hundred days, I think. One day we saw many bright colored birds flying.

"We are getting near land," said Don Columbus.

One night we were on the deck. It was getting late. I was just going to bed. Don Columbus jumped up quickly. He cried:

"A light! A light!" All the men came running.

Don Columbus had seen a light moving. He and many of the men did not go to sleep that night, but he made me go to bed.

The next day we saw land.

The men were not afraid any more. We got off the ship and went on the land. Don Columbus carried a flag with a Cross. He named the place San Salvador. This means Holy Savior. He named it for our Lord. Don Columbus had a great big

Cross put up. We all knelt down and thanked God and our Lady for letting us find land.

We saw some queer people. They had dark red skin. They wore feathers. They were kind to us. Don Columbus called them Indians. He asked them where the big cities were. They did not know.

The country was strange but very beautiful. There were strange birds of many colors, and strange fruits that I liked to eat. There were strange trees and plants. It was all so different from our country.

We stayed in this country some time. I had a nice time. Don Columbus let me play all I wanted.

I raise this Cross. I claim this land
For Isabella and Ferdinand!

III

Then one day he said we were **going** back. We took many of the strange things that we had found back with us. Even some of the Indians came with us.

We sailed and sailed for days and days.

Then we came to Palos again. All the people came out in the streets to see us. They were glad to see Don Columbus. They rang all the big bells.

I did not see the bad man who said he was my father.

We went to a big city. Don Columbus said to me, "We are going to see the King and Queen, Pedro, and maybe somebody else."

"Who is somebody else?" I asked.

Don Columbus looked at me and smiled. But he did not say anything.

He gave me beautiful clothes to wear.

We went to the palace of the King and Queen. There were many people in the palace. They were very nice to Don Columbus. I stood near a window and watched the people go past to talk to him. Once my heart came up into my mouth. A beautiful lady in rose color was near me. She was the beautiful lady of my dreams.

I walked right over to her. I did not know that I was doing this. Before I could think, I spoke. I said:

"Mother!"

I knew now that I had seen her before. I had called her "Mother" many times before.

She turned very white. She put out her hands. "Pedro," she cried. "Can it be Pedro?"

She took me in her arms and cried:
"My little son! My little son!"

It was really and truly my mother. I was the little boy the bad man had stolen. My mother told me this later. She said she knew me right away.

She took me to the big house and the lovely gardens.

It had not been just a dream. It was all true. I was her little son. Our Lady had given me my home and my mother again.

Our Lady and Don Columbus.

O lady with the lovely eyes,
Today you have had a glad surprise.

The Little Dove
of Our Lady

I

Around her head in the morning light
The little doves wreathed a halo bright.

The morning was cool and quiet. Soft gray clouds filled the sky. Little pink flowers covered the bushes by the big farm house. On the kitchen steps sat a little girl. She had a big apron tied around her neck. On her lap there was a big pan. In the pan was a cabbage. The little girl had a knife in her hand. She was cutting the cabbage to pieces. She heard a voice calling:

"Zoe, Zoe, have you fed the doves?"
The little girl called back:
"No, Mary Louise, not yet."
A minute later a tall girl came out the doorway. She had dark hair and eyes. She looked very much like Zoe. But Zoe's eyes were gray and her brown hair held many golden lights, like little sunbeams. Mary Louise was holding a pan of corn. She put the pan of corn on the steps.

Then she took Zoe's apron off and put the pan of cabbage in the kitchen.

"Come, little sister," she said. "We are going to feed the doves."

Zoe loved to go with Mary Louise to feed the doves. The doves were quite gentle and not at all afraid.

Mary Louise would let Zoe fill her hands with the grain and throw it to the birds. She would call to the birds, and soon they would be flying all around her. They would eat right out of her hand.

"There," said Zoe. She threw down the last handful. "O Mary Louise! Watch them fly. This is the way they do!"

Zoe stood on her toes and moved her arms up and down. She was laughing.

"Oh, I wish I could fly, too!"

Mary Louise smiled at her little sister.

"Oh, you can fly," she said.

Zoe's eyes got big.

"How?" she asked.

"Every little prayer that you say is just like one of these little doves. It flies on

shining white wings right up to Heaven. If you say many little prayers, then there are as many flying up to Heaven as there are doves in front of you now."

"Oh," said Zoe. Her eyes were even bigger than before.

Mary Louise put her arm around her little sister, and they went back to the kitchen.

Not long after this Zoe's dear mother became very ill. Soon she died. Poor little Zoe cried and cried and cried. Mary Louise tried to make her feel better, but she had a hard time doing so.

Once she found Zoe crying on the steps all by herself. She was saying over and over:

"I haven't any mother. I haven't any mother."

Mary Louise took her into the house. She led her to a very large and very beautiful picture of our Lady. She wiped Zoe's eyes. She said:

"Zoe, dear, it is true that God has taken our dear mother. But God has not left us without some one to take her place. See! There is a picture of God's own Mother. She is ours, too. She loves you very, very dearly. Talk to her, and ask her to take dear Mother's place."

Mary Louise then went softly out of the room.

Zoe looked into the beautiful eyes of our Lady. They seemed to smile at her. She stopped crying. She felt that our Lady was waiting for her to speak. She said:

"Blessed Mother, please take Mother's place."

And this wee prayer, like a little white dove with shining wings, flew straight up to our Lady's heart.

Mother of God, please be mine, too.
For oh! how much I do need you.

II

After this Zoe's father and Mary
Louise saw a change in little Zoe. She was
more gentle. She was kinder to her little
brothers. She asked Mary Louise if she
could go to Mass every morning with her.

Mary Louise was very glad to have little Zoe go with her.

They used to get up early and walk
down the beautiful country road to the
little Church. The birds were just waking.
The sky was getting pinker and brighter.
Zoe used to love this quiet morning walk.
She and Mary Louise would say their
Rosary as they walked along.

In the little Church, she would kneel,
oh, so quietly, at Mary Louise's side. She
loved to watch Mary Louise pray. It had
been Mary Louise who first taught her
what Holy Mass meant.

"Our Lord died on the Cross to save
our souls. The Holy Mass is just the same.
Our Lord on the Altar offers Himself to
His Eternal Father for us. You see, all

of us could not be with the Blessed Mother and Saint John when they stood at the foot of our Lord's Cross on the First Good Friday. And so He has given us the Holy Mass. It's the same."

Mary Louise taught Zoe to take care of the house. Of course, Zoe had to learn her lessons and go to school with her little brothers, too. But she was never selfish or lazy. She could cook and bake bread. She could sew. She knew just what to do in the house. Mary Louise was proud of her.

When evening came the children would watch for their father. They used to run to meet him.

Once Zoe's father said to her:

"You are not so noisy as you used to be. You are as gentle and lovely as one of your little white doves."

In Holy Mass God's grace is given;
It helps us on our way to Heaven.

III

Mary Louise had a secret, a big secret. She had had this secret a long time. Soon she would have to tell Zoe. At last a good chance came.

The two girls were on their way home from Mass. Zoe was a big girl now.

Mary Louise said:

"Zoe, do you love me very much?"

Zoe said:

"Mary Louise! you know there is nothing that I would not do for you."

"Yes," said Mary Louise. "I know that you love me. But real love often means doing something very hard. Zoe, I am going away."

Zoe was so surprised that she could not speak.

"Yes," Mary Louise went on, "I am going to be a Sister of Charity. You will have to take my place in the house. You will have to take care of Father and our brothers."

Big tears came into Zoe's eyes but still

she did not say anything. Mary Louise went on talking.

"You see, the Sisters of Charity give themselves to God. They do not spend all their lives praying in their houses. They go everywhere to help the poor and sick and little children. They go all over the world."

Mary Louise saw Zoe's tears.

"Just think," she said. "It is a lovely thing to always wear blue and white—our Lady's colors. And I shall wear on my head a cornette, a white bonnet with big white wings. I shall be like one of your

doves, Zoe. I shall fly to any one who needs my help.

A little smile came at last through Zoe's tears.

"It hurts, Mary Louise; it hurts very much! But I am really glad you are going," she said at last.

How nice to wear our Lady's blue,
And a big cornette with white wings, too.

74

IV

And so Mary Louise went. Of course, everybody missed her. She had been like sunshine in the house.

Now Zoe had to take care of the house. And she did it very well, too. She made her father and little brothers very happy.

Every day when she fed her doves she thought of Mary Louise. She knew that Mary Louise was very, very happy. Her letters said so.

Every day she went to Mass. She prayed for her father and Mary Louise and her brothers. She prayed for others, too, especially the poor and sick.

Zoe was very kind to the poor and sick. When she had time she used to go to see them and take them nice things. Everybody loved her.

One night Zoe had a dream. She dreamed that she was at Mass in the little Church. A strange old priest was saying the Mass. When the last prayer was finished, he turned around and walked over to her. She was frightened. She got up quickly and left the Church.

Then she woke up. She said to herself:

"That is strange! I wonder who that old priest could be!"

Then she went back to sleep again. And she had another dream.

She dreamed that she was in the house of a poor old woman whom she knew. She saw by the bedside of the sick woman the same old priest. He was looking at her. He seemed very kind. But Zoe was frightened again. She started to leave the house. This time the old priest spoke. He said:

"You run away from me now. But the day will come when you will be glad to come to me."

Zoe woke up again. This time the morning light was coming in the window.

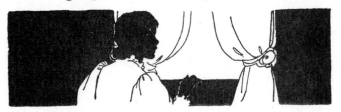

All that day and for many, many days
this dream stayed in Zoe's mind. She kept
wondering and wondering who the old
priest was. She knew that she had never
really met him. She wondered what he
wanted.

Not very long after this Zoe had a lovely trip. She went to see Mary Louise.
Mary Louise was now a Sister of Charity.
She wore the lovely dark blue dress and
the white winged cornette. She was Sister
Mary Louise. Zoe could hardly wait until
she got to the house. She rang the bell and
was taken to a big room to wait for Sister
Mary Louise—her dear Mary Louise.

While she was waiting she began to
look at the pictures on the walls.

Suddenly her eyes got very big. She
jumped up.

Yes indeed, it was true. She was looking at a picture of the old priest she had seen in her dreams. She saw the same kind face, the same smiling eyes, the same silver hair.

She heard a little noise in the hallway. She knew it was Mary Louise coming, but she could not take her eyes from the old priest. He seemed to be smiling at her.

"Zoe, Zoe," cried Mary Louise, putting her arms around her sister.

But Zoe only said:

"Mary Louise, who is that old priest?"

Mary Louise was surprised.

"That? Why that is a picture of our Holy Founder, the great Saint Vincent de Paul," she said.

Zoe seemed to think and think. Indeed, she was thinking very fast. Her heart began to sing as one of her little doves.

"I know, I know, I know. He is calling me to be one of his Sisters. I, too, shall wear our Lady's white and blue. I, too, shall wear the white winged cornette. I, too, shall go through the great, wide world taking care of God's poor."

A little prayer like a little white winged dove flew straight to God's Heart. She had said:

"Dear God, I thank You."

Then she turned around and kissed Sister Mary Louise. She was smiling.

Saint Vincent, please take care of me,
Wherever I may chance to be.

V

"Zoe," said her father, "what is the matter with you? You have been so very, very quiet since you went to see Mary Louise."

Now Zoe had wanted all along to tell her father everything. But she was afraid he would not let her go to be a Sister.

She knew she would have to tell him sometime. So she said to herself:

"I shall tell Father now."

She said to her father:

"I will tell you, Father. I want to be a Sister of Charity like Mary Louise. Please let me go."

She knew her father loved her, oh, so much. What would he say?

"No," he said. "I shall not let you go. It was hard enough to give up Mary Louise, but I cannot give you up."

Then he went out of the room.

Poor Zoe! She cried, and she prayed. But her father would not change his mind.

One day he said to her:

"I am going to send you to the big city of Paris. If you go there, you will not want to be a Sister any more."

Zoe did not want to go to Paris, but she went for awhile to please her father. When she came home, he found out that she still wanted to be a Sister. But he would not give in. He sent her to a big school for awhile.

"Now she will forget," he said.

But Zoe did not forget.

The Head of the School, wrote to her father.

She said:

"Your daughter Zoe is not happy here. You had better let her come home."

And so Zoe found herself once more at home.

One day her father said to her:

"Zoe, I cannot understand why you want to go away and be a Sister."

Zoe was standing by the window looking out. She said:

"Father, do you see all those sheep coming down the road?"

Her father looked out the window. He saw a great number of sheep coming down the road. Several shepherd boys were with them. All these sheep belonged to him.

"Yes, Zoe," he said.

"Father," she went on, "don't you understand? Suppose those sheep were left to take care of themselves. What would happen?"

"Many things," said her father. "Some

would get hurt. Some would get lost and never find their way home. Some would go into the woods, and the wolves would eat them. That is why they need the care of the shepherd boys."

"Father," said Zoe, "It is just the same with people. They are God's sheep. They need shepherds, too. They need many Priests and Sisters to help them save their souls. If they are left alone, they forget God. They forget the way home to Heaven. Their souls get hurt by the black sins. Souls, too, can get lost and killed.

"Father, let me go?"

It was very still in the room for about a minute. Then Zoe's father put his arms around her.

"My little dove," he said. "I have made your home a cage. But now I shall open the door and let you fly away."

Zoe put her arms around her father's neck.

"God bless you, little dove of our Lady!" he said.

Then he kissed her.

I thank You, God for all You do;
Thanks for all Priests and Sisters, too.

I Want to Be a Sister

The Great Gift
of Our Lady

I

She works, she talks, she laughs, she prays,
Through all her Seminary days.

Ding! Dong! Ding! Dong! The great
bell rang.

Then through the long white hallways
of the Mother House of the Daughters of
Charity in Paris came the sound of many
footsteps. Many young girls were going
through the halls. Each of them wore a
dress of soft black with a little white
shawl carefully pinned in front. Each of
them wore a little white cap that came
out a little over her face.

All of them went into a large room. There were many seats in this room. At one end of the room there was a statue of our Lady.

First the young girls knelt down and said a "Hail Mary." Then they sat down. They began to sew. They talked and laughed while they sewed.

All of these young girls were Seminary Sisters. They were in the Mother House in Paris. They were learning how to be Sisters of Charity. In a few months they would receive the beautiful blue dress and lovely white cornette. Then they would be sent out anywhere in the wide world to help the poor and the sick and the little children.

These young girls had come from many places. Some had come from far, far away. One of them was Zoe. But she was not called Zoe now. Now she was Sister Catherine.

After awhile a Sister of Charity came in the room. Her name was Sister Martha.

She talked to the Sisters every day. She

taught them how to be Sisters of Charity.
She taught them how to take care of the
poor and the sick and children.

Today, Sister Martha talked to them
about our Blessed Mother.

She said:

"Our Blessed Lady is God's Mother. He
loved her so much that He has made her
Queen of Heaven. She is Queen of the
Angels and Queen of the Saints. But she
is our Queen too. She is more than our
Queen. She is our Mother. She loves us as
her children. She watches over us."

Zoe was listening, but she was thinking, too, of the time her own dear mother
died. She was thinking of how she had
asked our Lady to be her mother. Sister
Catherine loved our Lady, oh, so dearly!

Sister Catherine had always wanted to

see our Blessed Lady and talk to her. When she had been little, she had often asked her sister Mary Louise how soon she could see our Blessed Mother. Mary Louise would say:

"When you get to Heaven, Zoe."

And Zoe would say:

"That is a long, long time to wait. Can't I see her before that?"

And she had often asked her Guardian Angel to please ask our Lady to come down on earth to see her.

Today, in the Seminary, Sister Catherine was listening and thinking of all these things. She said to herself:

"I am going to ask again. Maybe if I pray very hard to St. Vincent and my Guardian Angel, our Lady will come."

Oh, could I see our Lady dear!
My Guardian Angel, bring her here!

II

Night came. All was still in the great
Mother House. Everybody was in bed,
asleep. The big clock over the Chapel
struck nine, ten, eleven. Everything was
as still as could be. Half-past eleven
came. Sister Catherine awoke. Someone
was calling her. She heard a sweet voice
calling: "Sister, Sister, Sister."

Sister Catherine sat up in bed. There
were soft white curtains all around the
bed, so she could not see anyone. She
leaned over and pulled the curtain back.
Oh, what do you think she saw? At first
she thought she was dreaming. But she
was not dreaming. She was wide awake.

There by her bed stood a beautiful
child, robed in shining white. He had
beautiful blue eyes and soft golden curls.
He seemed about five years old. There
was a bright light shining all around his
head. He was her Guardian Angel.

"Come," he said. "The Blessed Virgin
is waiting for you. Come to the Chapel."

Sister Catherine thought to herself:

"If I get up, I shall wake up the other Sisters."

She only thought this. But the Angel knew what she was thinking. He said:

"No, they will not wake up. Get dressed quickly. I am waiting for you."

Sister Catherine dressed very quickly. The Angel led her out in the hall and down the stairs. The halls and the stairs were bright with light.

Sister Catherine was much surprised.

They came to the Chapel now. It was locked. The Angel put his hand on the door, and it opened right away.

They went in the Chapel. Sister Catherine's eyes were getting bigger and bigger. For the Chapel was all lighted up. The Altar looked as it did on Christmas. It was so bright and beautiful.

They went up close to the Altar steps, near a big arm chair. But Sister Catherine did not see the Blessed Virgin. It was very, very quiet. Then the great clock struck: one, two, three, four, five, six, seven, eight, nine, ten, eleven, twelve!

The Angel said softly:

"Here comes the Blessed Virgin."

Sister Catherine heard a little noise. She thought it sounded like a silk dress moving. She looked up. Our Lady was standing before her.

Then our Blessed Lady sat down in the big arm chair. She looked at Sister Catherine and smiled at her, oh, so sweetly.

Sister Catherine fell on her knees by our Lady's side. She rested her hands on our Lady's knee.

At last, Sister Catherine had seen our Lady. Now she could talk to her. Oh, how happy she was! Our Lady talked to Sister

It Is Mary, the Mother of God

Catherine for some time. Once she said:

"My child, God wants you to do something for Him. You will know what it is a little later."

Sister Catherine was glad to hear that she could do something for God.

For nearly two whole hours Our Lady stayed and talked to Sister Catherine. Sister Catherine looked at our Lady's beautiful face. She kept saying over and over to herself:

"It is Mary, the Mother of God, and my Mother."

She wished she could stay at our Lady's side forever!

But at last our Lady went. The little Angel said to Sister Catherine:

"She is gone."

He led her back to her bed again. Then he, too, went away. Everything was dark and quiet. Sister Catherine got in bed. She heard the clock strike two. But she could not go to sleep. She said over and over to herself:

"Oh! I have seen our Lady. I have

talked with her! How wonderful she was!"

'Twas in the middle of the night,
She saw a little Angel bright.

III

The happy days came and went. They went very fast. But still Sister Catherine did not know what it was that God wanted her to do.

Summer was over. The leaves were nearly all off the trees. It was getting cold. And still Sister Catherine waited.

"Maybe I will know by Christmas," she said to herself.

But she did not have to wait until Christmas.

It was the twenty-seventh of November. It was Saturday evening. All the

Sisters had gone in the Chapel at half past five o'clock. Everything, of course, was very still. All the Sisters were kneeling and looking at the Altar. God was there in the Blessed Sacrament.

Sister Catherine was thinking about our Blessed Lady. She said to our Lord:

"Will it be much longer before I know what You want me to do?"

Just at that very minute she heard a sound like moving silk. The sound seemed to come from near St. Joseph's Altar. Sister Catherine looked over that way.

There stood our Lady! Oh, how beautiful she was! Her robe was the color of the early morning sky. Over her head was a long, soft, white veil. She was standing on a big ball. There were some clouds

around it. She was looking up to Heaven. In her hands she held a ball. It looked like the world. She was offering the world to God. She was praying for it.

On our Lady's fingers were many rings. The rings were full of very, very bright stones. Rays of light came from these stones. The rays fell to our Lady's feet.

Sister Catherine heard a voice. The voice said:

"These rays mean the graces our Blessed Mother gives to all who ask for them. Some of the stones do not send out any rays. This means that some people do not get graces because they do not ask for them."

Sister Catherine just knelt there looking and looking at our Lady.

Then she saw our Lady looking at her very sweetly. Sister Catherine heard the voice again. The voice said:

"The ball in our Lady's hands means that she prays for everybody's soul."

Then Sister Catherine did not see the ball any more. Our Lady lowered her arms. The rays became brighter and brighter.

Then Sister Catherine saw words written around our Lady's head. The words were:

"O Mary, conceived without sin, pray for us who have recourse to thee."

Then a frame of gold seemed to be around our Lady and the words. Sister Catherine seemed to be looking at a beautiful picture.

Sister Catherine heard the voice again. The voice said:

"Have a Medal made to look like what you are seeing. Everybody who wears it will receive great graces. It should be worn around the neck."

The picture turned. Sister Catherine

The Miraculous Medal

saw many things on the back. She saw a big letter M. This meant Mary, our Lady's name.

Below the letter M were the Sacred Hearts of Jesus and Mary. Above the M and a little higher up, was a Cross. Around all these were twelve bright stars.

Then Sister Catherine saw the picture no more. It was gone, just like a light that had been put out.

But Sister Catherine's heart was singing. It was singing as it did when she had found out that she was to be a Sister.

"I know, I know, I know," her heart sang. "This is what God wishes me to do. I am to have this Medal made, so that everybody will love our Lady more and more."

She saw our Lady standing there,
The golden rays fell everywhere.

IV

Sister Catherine knew that she had a big secret. It was a secret that belonged to God and our Lady. There was only one person to whom she could tell it. And that was Father Aladel. Sister Catherine knew that Father Aladel would have to have the beautiful Medal of our Lady made.

So she went to him. She told him all about what she had seen. She told him that our Lady wanted him to have the Medal made.

Father was much surprised. But he did not have our Lady's Medal made right away.

One day Sister Catherine was praying to our Lady.

She said:

"It isn't my fault, Blessed Mother, that your beautiful Medal isn't made yet! I told Father, but he has not done anything about it."

Our Blessed Lady said:

"He will have my Medal made. He loves

me very dearly. He would not do anything that I do not like."

And so at last the beautiful Medal was
made. Two thousand of them!

On the front side was our Lady standing on the world. She was holding out her
hands. Rays of light were falling from
them. Around her were the words:

"O Mary, conceived without sin, pray
for us who have recourse to thee!"

On the back was the letter M, the Sacred Hearts of Jesus and Mary and the Cross. Around all these were twelve stars. These Medals were given to all the Sisters. They were told to give them to the poor sick and little children.

Sister Catherine kissed hers again and again.

"Yes, we must give everybody a Medal," she said. "Everybody must love our Lady more and more. And our Lady will give to those who wear her beautiful Medal, very many graces."

A Medal like this you shall make.
And all should wear it for my sake.

V

Just at this time, very many people in Paris were quite sick. Many were dying. The doctors were not able to save all the people.

The Sisters of Charity went to see the poor, sick people. They put the beautiful Medal of our Lady around their necks. They said to the people:

"Our Blessed Mother brought this Medal from Heaven. She gave it to one of our Sisters. Our Lady says that you should wear it around your neck. You should say the little prayer on it. If you wear this Medal for love of our Lady, she will give you great graces.

"Say the little prayer on it with me."

Then the poor, sick person would say the little prayer.

"O Mary, conceived without sin, pray for us who have recourse to thee."

Our Lady heard their prayers. The sick people who wore her Medal got well. Those who had been very bad became

good. They were sorry for their sins. They went to Confession. Their black souls were made white again. They received Holy Communion. Our Lord came into their hearts. They were very good from that time on. Everybody said:

"What a beautiful Medal! Our Lady gives great graces to those who wear it. We will wear it all the time!"

They said, too:

"Our Lady is working many miracles through her beautiful Medal. She makes sick people well. She makes bad people good again. Her Medal is Miraculous. We shall call it the Miraculous Medal."

And all this was true. Our Lady was working many miracles through her beautiful Medal. She was making the sick well again, and the bad people good.

A miracle is something very great that God does, or that He lets His Mother or the Saints do. A miracle is something very wonderful. Our Lord worked many miracles when He was on earth. He raised the dead to life. Only God can do that. He fed thousands of people with five little loaves of bread and two little fishes. Only God could do that.

God let our Lady work many, many miracles for the people who loved her Medal.

The sick get well, the bad get good,
Just as our Lady said they would.

VI

"To whom did our Lady give this beautiful Miraculous Medal?"

Everybody was asking this question. Even the Sisters of Charity asked this question. Nobody seemed to be able to tell them.

Only three people knew the big secret. And these three were Sister Catherine, Father Aladel, and the good Archbishop of Paris. And they did not tell. Very often the Sisters would try to guess which Sister had seen our Lady. Some of them thought that it was Sister Catherine. But they could not be sure of this.

And just what was Sister Catherine doing all this time?

She had received the beautiful blue

and white dress of a Sister of Charity. She had been sent to a big hospital. There were many poor, sick people in this hospital. Sister Catherine took care of the kitchen. She saw that everybody had nice things to eat. She saw that everybody had enough.

Sister Catherine saw that the chickens were cared for. Every day she went out to feed them. She liked to feed the chickens. They made her think of the doves she had fed when she had been a little girl.

There were many old men in this hospital. Sister Catherine was very kind to them all. She gave each one a Miraculous Medal. She taught them to say the little prayer on the Miraculous Medal.

"O Mary, conceived without sin, pray for us who have recourse to thee."

But Sister Catherine was not proud. She did not want people to notice her. She did not tell them that she had seen our Lady.

She knew she had a great big secret. And she kept her big secret, too.

She was always quiet and gentle, like one of her little doves.

At last the happiest day of her life came. She was going to Heaven!

Her beautiful soul flew up to God and our Lady, like a dove with wings of shining white.

O Dove of our Lady, pray that we
May love our Medal just like thee.

VII

A hundred years have passed since our dear Lady told Sister Catherine to have her beautiful Miraculous Medal made.

Now all good Catholics through the great, wide world wear the Miraculous Medal. They know that our Lady wishes them to wear her Medal. They know that our Lady promised great graces to those who would wear it in her honor.

Mothers put it on their little babies. Boys and girls wear it in school and out of school. Soldiers wear it on the battle fields. Sailors wear it on the great seas. Men who fly in airplanes wear it when they are high above the clouds. We are told that Lindbergh had a Miraculous Medal when he flew across the ocean.

Sisters wear it on their breasts and on

their rosaries. Priests and Bishops, and our Holy Father the Pope love and wear the Miraculous Medal.

They all say that beautiful prayer:

"O Mary, conceived without sin, pray for us who have recourse to thee.

* * *

And from her Throne in Heaven Mary looks down on earth. All the Angels and Saints around her Throne look down on earth, too.

They see everybody in the world—in America, in China and in Africa, everywhere. They see very, very, very many who wear around their necks something small and beautiful and shining.

Our Lady smiles on these people. She says to the Angels and Saints:

"Look! See all those little babies and boys and girls and men and women. You must take good care of them, for I love them very, very dearly. They are my special children. For they are wearing a Miraculous Medal."

Then she says:

"This is how I bless them."

She holds out her beautiful hands, and brightest rays of golden light fall from them. The golden rays fall upon those who wear the Medal.

Our Lady is shedding graces on her children who wear her Medal, as she told Blessed Catherine she would a hundred years ago.

The Miraculous Medal I shall wear
And often say the little prayer,
O Mary, conceived without sin, pray
for us who have recourse to thee.

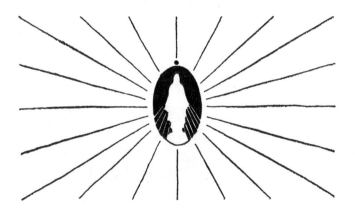

Black Robe

"Tell me where the Indians are."
"They live in America—oh, so far."

Little Isaac Jogues stood looking out the window. The rain was falling. He was tired of playing alone. He did not know what to do. He could not go out to play. His mother came into the room and sat down by the table. She had some sewing in her hand. Isaac ran over to her:

"I wish I could go out to play," he said. "I am tired of my toys."

His mother said:

"Only little Indians play in the rain."

"Indians?" said Isaac. "What are Indians?" He sat down on a low seat by his mother.

"The Indians are people who live far, far away," said his mother. "They live across the wide, wide sea. They are not white as we are. They are called Redskins because their skin looks dark red. They live in big woods. They do not live in nice houses as we do.

"They love to hunt in the woods. They shoot with bows and arrows." She stopped.

"Please go on," said Isaac.

Mrs. Jogues put down her sewing. She picked up a pen and some paper. She drew a little picture.

"They live in little houses like this," she said—

"These are wigwams.

"Their bows and arrows look like this"—

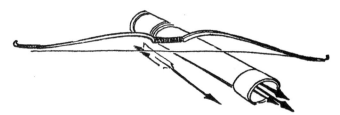

The rain was still falling, but Isaac had forgotten all about the rain. He was watching his mother's fingers move over the paper.

"The Indians are tall and strong. They paint their faces with bright colors. They wear feathers in their hair, like this—

"They go hunting in the big woods. They kill bears and foxes and deer. They wear the skins of the bears and deer.

They can swim and fish. They make boats called canoes."

"That is nice," said Isaac. "I think I would like to be an Indian."

"But the Indians are not good. They steal and lie," said his mother. "They are cruel. They hunt people they don't like, and if they catch them they are very mean to them. They tie the poor things to big stakes, and build big fires around them. Then they dance and sing around them while they are burning."

"All that is bad," said Isaac. "They should tell it in Confession and not do it any more."

"They can't go to Confession," said his mother. "At least most of them. There are not many priests over in America where the Indians live. These very Indians have no one to tell them about God and our Blessed Lady."

Isaac's big brown eyes looked very hard at the paper.

"I am sorry," said Isaac. "Those Indians ought to have priests. Do you think that

God would send them a priest if we asked Him?"

Mrs. Jogues' fingers began to move very fast over the paper. "Like this—"

"Here are the Indians and here is the priest teaching them to be good. Yes, Isaac, we will ask God to send a priest to the Indians who are the very worst of all."

Most are bad, though some are good;
They need a priest, in the deep, dark wood.

II

When Isaac was ten years old, he went away to school to the Jesuit Fathers and studied his lessons very well. He prayed well. He often wrote to his dear mother. His mother was very glad when his letters came. She was so glad when the Jesuit Father wrote nice things about Isaac.

The Jesuit Fathers have many schools for boys, but that is not all they do. They go to many parts of the world. They teach the poor pagans like the Chinese and the black people about God.

Isaac met many of the Jesuit priests who had sailed over great seas and had been in far countries. They told him many strange things that they had seen and heard. They told him how they had taught poor pagans about God.

Isaac said one day:

"I think that it is a very great thing to go far away and teach poor pagans about God. I want to be a priest. I want to go to the poor black people far, far away in Africa. I am going to pray very hard. I know our Blessed Mother will get me this grace."

And so Isaac studied harder than ever. He prayed very much. He wrote to his dear mother and told her that he wanted to be a priest. When this letter came she was very happy. She wrote to him and said:

"I hope and pray that you will be a priest. I hope that I shall be in the church when you say your first Mass. I hope I will be the first one to receive Holy Communion from your hands. Your hands will be very holy then. They will touch God. I shall kiss them the day of your first Mass."

These days were very happy for Isaac. He met more of the priests. Some of them had been in the American forests with the Indians. They told him many things about the Indians.

One day he was talking about the black pagans. He said he was going to help them. A priest who heard him said:

"No, you will not go to the black people. You will go to your poor red brothers and sisters in America."

Isaac thought about this very much.

Then he prayed to know God's Holy Will.
And God let him know that he should go
to the Indians.

Unto the Indians I shall go,
And teach them our good God to know.

III

At last the great day came when Isaac Jogues was made a priest. Now he could say Mass; he could forgive sins; he could baptize; he could give people Holy Communion. He was very happy. He was Father Jogues now. He thanked God and our Lady for letting him be a priest.

The great day of his First Mass came. His dear mother was there. She saw him stand at the altar. She heard the little bell ring. She saw him bow his head. She saw him raise the shining white Host. She knew his holy hands were touching our Lord. She was so happy. She said:

"O God, I thank you for letting my boy be a holy priest."

The little bell rang again. The people went up to receive Holy Communion. His mother was first. She was the very first one to receive our Lord from the holy hands of her son.

After Mass, Father Jogues talked to his mother. He said:

"Do you remember one rainy day when I was a little boy? You told me about the Indians and made me little pictures of them?"

Mrs. Jogues said, "Yes, my son, I remember."

"Do you remember, Mother, how you told me that they were bad? You told me that they didn't know anything about God?"

"Yes, my son," she said, "I remember."

"Do you remember, Mother, that I felt

sorry for the poor Indians? I asked you
if God would send a priest to the very
worst ones if we prayed to Him? You
made a little picture of many Indians
sitting on the ground and a priest standing near talking to them about God. You
said, 'We will pray to God to send a priest
to the very worst ones!' Mother, I am that
priest. God wants me to go to them."

Big tears came into his mother's eyes.
She cried, "O Isaac, my son, how can I
give you up? America is so far, far away;
and the Indians are so cruel!"

She took hold of his hands and kissed
them.

"These hands belong to God now," said
Father Jogues. "They must lift the Holy
Host in the deep forests of America. They

must pour the holy waters of Baptism over the poor red brothers and sisters. They must be raised in absolution over the bad ones who are sorry for their sins. It is the Will of God."

"You are right, my son," said his mother. She did not cry any more. She kissed his holy hands again and said:

"O God, these holy hands of my son are Yours. May they do great things for You."

My hands are Yours; my heart is, too;
Oh, may they do great things for You.

IV

On a big ship, with sails like great white wings, Father Jogues stood. And the big ship moved over the deep, green waters, week after week. At last they came to America. Father Jogues saw Indians for the first time. He was very glad. He said to himself:

"It is just like a dream come true."

For seven years, Father Jogues lived with the Indians. He ate the same kind of food that they did, he lived in the same kind of house. He went far, far through the deep woods. He loved the deep, quiet woods. He loved the great rushing rivers and the silver lakes. He loved all the many beautiful wild flowers. They made

him think of God and Heaven. He said:

"If earth is so beautiful, what is Heaven like?"

And when the winters came and the snows made everything white he would say:

"O God, help me to make the souls of the poor Indians as white as this snow."

But most of all he loved the poor Indians. They called him Black Robe. He worked very hard to save their souls. It was to please them, he ate the same kind of food as they did, and lived in the same kind of house. He did not like the food. At first it made him sick, but God helped him.

He went from one place to another. He

met many Indians. He taught them about God. He showed them how to be good. These Indians wanted to be good. They said:

"Black Robe, we will do as you say. We will not be bad any more."

Father Jogues baptized many, many Indians. He taught them how to go to Confession. He let them make their First Holy Communion. They came to Mass. They loved our Lady.

Sometimes he had to go through the deep woods for days. Sometimes he went in a canoe up the rivers or lakes for many, many miles. He did this because he wanted to teach as many Indians as he could. In summer it was hard. But in winter it was much harder. It was very cold. Father Jogues and the Indians who showed him the way had to go on snow-shoes.

Once they got lost in the woods. They only had one little piece of bread left. But Father Jogues did not mind, he said:

"God will take care of us."

They built a little house with branches
of trees. They made a big fire. Then they
said their prayers and went to sleep. In
the morning they asked our Lady to help
them. They went on and on. Soon they
came to a little Indian village. The Indians were very glad to see Black Robe.
He baptized a poor dying woman here.

Father Jogues used to spend all his free
time in prayer. He prayed before our
Lord in the Blessed Sacrament. He said
to our Lord:

"Please let me lay down my life for love

of You, to prove my true love for You."

He said this prayer many times. One day, after he had said this prayer, he heard our Lord speak to him. Our Lord said:

"You shall have what you asked for. Be brave and strong."

Father Jogues was very happy.

V

Not long after this, Father Jogues and a friend named Rene were going up a river with some of the good Indians. Rene was a young Doctor. They met some other Indians who shot arrows at them. They fired guns, too. Father Jogues knew that these were the Mohawks. They were bad Indians — the very worst of all. The Mohawks beat the good Indians. They tied them with ropes. They were very cruel to them. They took everything in the canoes. They took Father Jogues and the rest of them to their home. All the bad Indians stood in two lines. Each one had a big club. They made the good Indians and Father Jogues walk between them. Then all the Mohawks hit them with their clubs. One of the Indians cut off Father Jogues' right thumb. The pain was very great. Father Jogues was very brave. Now he could not say Mass any more.

Father Jogues became a slave. They

did not give him enough to eat. They did not give him enough to wear. They made him work very hard. They did not like to see him pray. They killed nearly all the good Indians.

Father Jogues still had his friend, Rene. Rene loved the children. He wanted to teach them about God.

One day an old Indian saw Rene talking to his little grandson. He saw Rene showing the little boy how to make the Sign of the Cross. He was very angry. He told a young Indian to kill Rene. The young Indian went to look for Rene. He found Father Jogues and Rene taking a walk. They were saying the Rosary. The young Indian hit Rene on the head with a hatchet. Rene cried out, "Jesus!" and fell on the ground dead.

Father Jogues was very sad after Rene died. Of course, he was very, very glad that Rene was in Heaven, but Father Jogues was very lonesome. He used to go out into the woods and cut the Holy Name of Jesus on the trees. Sometimes he would cut a big Cross.

One day Father Jogues got away. He went on a boat down the river to the big city of New York. Here he met kind people who helped him. He got on a big ship and went back to France.

O Holy Name of "Jesus"! be
A prayer I often say to Thee.

VI

Everybody was glad to see him. The good Queen asked to see him. She cried when she saw his poor hands. She said:

"God thinks they are more beautiful now than they ever were before."

Our Holy Father the Pope told him that he could say Mass, even if his hands had been so badly hurt. That pleased Father Jogues more than anything else.

Father Jogues did not stay in France very long. He said:

"I must go back to my poor Indians. I have not made them love God yet."

And so he came back to America. He came back to the bad Mohawks.

Some of the Mohawks began to listen to him, but others did not like him at all. At last some very bad ones made up their minds to kill him. They asked him to come to dinner. Father Jogues felt that he was going to be killed that day. He was very glad. He thanked God.

Two bad Indians came to take him to

the dinner. They walked with him to the door. Just as he was going in the doorway, one of the Indians hit him on the head with a sharp hatchet. He said, "Jesus! Jesus!" and fell dead upon the ground.

The bad Indians cut off his head and put it on a pole so that everybody could see it.

Father Jogues was a very great and a very holy priest. Now the Church says we are to call him Saint Isaac Jogues.

Not very far from the city of Albany in New York is the place where St. Isaac Jogues gave his life for God and the poor Indians. Today there is a beautiful

Church on the spot. Hundreds and hundreds of men and women and children go to that beautiful place. They think of all Father Jogues did for God. They ask him to help them be brave and good and love God as he did. They say:

"Saint Isaac Jogues pray for us!"

Maybe some day you, too, will go to that holy place. But even if you can't go yet, you can talk to dear Father Jogues. You, too, can say:

"Dear Saint Isaac Jogues, help me to be brave and good."

To Auriesville some day I'll go,
And pray to him who loved You so.

Oh blessed were the sandals
    That kissed our Lady's feet,
And shielded them from any hurt
    Whene'er they walked the street.
I am not worthy, Mary sweet,
    To kiss the dust beneath thy feet;
But shall a little sandal be
    A greater help, than I, to thee?

INDEX